The World's Greatest Trails

Diana Noonan

Contents

Walking Trails Around the World

Many people enjoy walking in the wild with a backpack on their backs. In the USA, it is called "hiking". In New Zealand, it is called "tramping". Australians often call it "bushwalking", and in the UK it is called "hillwalking", "hiking" or "rambling". There are some exciting (and very famous) walking trails to explore in different parts of the world.

Hikers walk on the famous Kungsleden Trail in Sweden.

The Appalachian Trail the USA

One of the most famous hiking routes in the USA is the Appalachian Trail (say: *a-puh-la-chuhn*). It follows the Appalachian Mountains through 14 states, from Georgia to Maine. At 3518 kilometres long, it is one of the longest trails in the world. The idea for the trail came from a hiker named Benton MacKaye. He wanted people from cities to have a special place where they could enjoy nature.

The Appalachian Trail is located in eastern USA.

People who **through-hike** the trail take between 5 and 7 months to complete their journey. Most through-hikers start in the south and aim to complete their hike before Baxter State Park, in the state of Maine, closes for winter. Two to three million people each year enjoy hiking parts of the trail on shorter day or overnight trips.

A hiker stops to survey the Appalachian Trail.

There are shelters situated along the Appalachian Trail.

The Appalachian Trail includes more than 350 **peaks** that are over 1500 metres high. It also has deep **gorges** filled with waterfalls, maple forests and crystal-clear lakes. Along the trail, hikers see all kinds of wildlife, from foxes and raccoons to white-tailed deer and moose. Many people walk sections of the trail during springtime, when different kinds of flowering trees, such as dogwoods and tulip trees, are in bloom.

There are plenty of places to sleep for the night on most sections of the Appalachian Trail. The route winds through the middle of many towns, and crosses a road every 6.4 kilometres on average. On many sections of the trail, there are also campsites, mountain huts and simple shelters. Volunteers living in towns closest to the shelters help take care of them. Hikers help look after their sleeping sites by carrying out any waste they bring with them on the trail, such as cans and paper.

Bears live along many parts of the trail, but a bear encounter is rare. Hikers try to make plenty of noise as they walk along, so that they don't come upon a bear suddenly and frighten it into protecting itself. Bears are attracted to the smell of food, so hikers are careful to follow instructions and hoist their belongings, especially food, into a tree well away from their campsite.
A common danger on the Appalachian Trail is the poison ivy plant. If it touches the skin, it can cause painful blisters.

Think and Talk About ...

The area surrounding the Appalachian Trail is of great significance to Native Americans.

It can snow along some parts of the Appalachian Trail at any time of the year.

People need to be prepared for all kinds of weather when hiking the Appalachian Trail, especially in the north, where snow can fall in any month of the year. Becoming too hot is just as dangerous as becoming too cold, so hikers pack clothing to suit all conditions. In severe weather, lightning can also be a **hazard**, and if hikers in exposed areas are caught out in a storm, they should seek shelter.

Getting lost in the outdoors is always a danger, but Appalachian Trail hikers have a system of **paint blazes** to help them find the trail. White paint blazes 5 centimetres wide and 15 centimetres high mark the Appalachian Trail. In mountainous sections, wooden posts and **cairns** help mark the route.

The Pennine Way the UK

One of the most famous walking trails in the United Kingdom is the Pennine Way. This trail is 429 kilometres long and runs from northern England to just over the border of Scotland. Pennine Way walkers can look forward to some interesting experiences on their trip. The trail is full of history, including the remains of Hadrian's Wall, a stone wall built by the Romans almost 2000 years ago. There are old mines, historic buildings and the ruins of villages to see on this trail.

N
0 20 40 60 80 100
KILOMETRES
the Pennine Way
SCOTLAND
Newcastle upon Tyne
North Pennines
ENGLAND
York
South Pennines
Leeds
Manchester
Peak District

The Pennine Way is located in the UK.

Every year, thousands of people walk the whole distance. Hundreds of thousands of people walk parts of it. Fit walkers take between 16 and 19 days to complete the whole trail but, in 1989, Mike Hartley ran the Pennine Way in two days, 17 hours, 20 minutes and 15 seconds. This record-setter did not sleep during this time, but he did stop for two 18-minute breaks. One of his breaks was for a meal of fish and chips!

The remains of Hadrian's Wall can be seen along the Pennine Way.

The valley known as High Cup Nick
is a stunning sight.

Along the Pennine Way, there are many animals to look out for. Some are farm animals, including sheep and cows. Others, such as bats, red squirrel and deer, are wild. If a walker is lucky, they may catch a glimpse of an Arctic hare. In summer, these hares are usually brown and grey, but in the winter, their fur turns snowy white to match the winter landscape.

Pennine Way walkers can expect to see gushing waterfalls, such as Cauldron Snout, cliffs, caves and strange limestone formations. They will cross the treeless **moorland** of Kinder Scout and look out over the deep U-shaped valley known as High Cup Nick.

The Pennine Way passes close to towns and villages. Some walkers stay at hotels and hostels for the night. Others take their tents and stay at camping grounds. There is a **bothy** on the way, which people can sleep in, but its beds are often occupied quickly. Walkers who want a good rest need to plan their trip carefully and book ahead to make sure they have somewhere to sleep for the night.

There are no dangerous animals along the Pennine Way, but walkers do have to be prepared for extremes of weather. Most people walk the trail in summer, but many parts of the Pennine Way are high and exposed. Strong winds, hot sun, heavy rain and sub-zero temperatures can occur at any time. In winter, there may be snow. In fog or mist, it is possible to not notice the trail markers and lose the way.

Hikers on the Pennine Way should always be prepared for poor weather.

Think and Talk About ...

The Pennine Way is known as one of Britain's toughest walking trails.

Walkers should wear strong shoes and boots, even if they are only on a Pennine Way day walk. They need to pack clothes for all weather, no matter what time of year they are on the trail. Clean water is not always available, so walkers should carry their own, as well as emergency food supplies. A map and compass (and knowing how to use them) are important because mobile phone coverage is not always available on the Pennine Way. A first-aid kit, whistle and survival bag are useful in emergencies. Walkers should always tell a friend where they plan to go and when they expect to return.

The Tongariro Crossing New Zealand

One of the most popular trails in New Zealand is the 19.4-kilometre Tongariro Crossing. This trail across a **volcanic** landscape takes 7 to 8 hours to finish. Most of the 60 000 people who tramp it each year enjoy the trail as a day walk. They use the trail in the warmer months of spring to autumn. Unless trampers are experienced, they will need to take a guide with them in winter.

NEW ZEALAND
Mt Tongariro
1967 m
Mangatepopo
Mt Ngauruhoe
2287 m
N
0 1 2 3 4 5
KILOMETRES
the Tongariro Crossing

The Tongariro Crossing is located in New Zealand.

Hikers on the Tongariro Crossing view spectacular scenery.

The Tongariro Crossing winds its way over an area of **active** volcanoes, so there is plenty to see. Trampers actually cross a volcanic crater: the desert-like South Crater of Mt Tongariro. Unless it is cloudy, the cone-shaped, 2287-metre high Mt Ngauruhoe is the volcano most people notice first. Strong trampers climb it as a side trip.

Along the way, there are bubbling streams, views of old lava flows and bright-emerald lakes. Trampers walk over rocks once thrown out of erupting volcanoes.

Mountain flowers, such as buttercups and daisies, can be seen on the trail in summer. Lucky trampers may spot a native falcon soaring through the sky or a North Island robin in the trees below the bushline.

Most people make the Tongariro Crossing in one day and enjoy a short break at Ketetahi Hut. The hut is a place to fill water bottles and escape the weather. The hut has bunk beds, so trampers who want to stay overnight have a place to sleep. If the weather is fine, trampers usually take another break at a **scenic** spot, such as Red Crater.

Only experienced hikers should attempt the Tongariro Crossing in winter.

Think and Talk About ...

Some parts of the *Lord of the Rings* movies were filmed on the Tongariro Crossing.

There are no wild animals to concern trampers on the Tongariro Crossing, but volcanoes can be a problem. Trampers need to check with the Department of Conservation before they begin their trip, to make sure the volcanoes are not rumbling or erupting. If volcanic activity suddenly occurs while trampers are on the trail, they should look out for flying ash and rocks, scalding steam and poisonous gases.

Sudden weather changes are also a danger. The day may be sunny and warm in the car park where the trail begins, but it may be snowing or blowing a **gale** 1000 metres further up the mountain. Low cloud can make finding trail markers a problem.

Trampers on the Tongariro Crossing may be making the journey in just one day, but they still need to come well prepared. Cold-weather clothes and emergency food and water should be carried, even if the weather forecast is good. In hot weather, sunglasses, sunscreen and a sun hat are important. Mobile phone coverage is reasonably good for much of the trail, so at least one person per group should carry a phone. A map and compass are important when mist or low cloud makes it difficult to see trail markers.

Trampers need to be aware of signs of volcanic ash, which can be a danger on the Tongariro Crossing.

The Overland Track Australia

One of the best-known trails in Australia is the Overland Track. It crosses a rugged mountain area in Tasmania. The 73-kilometre-long trail takes up to six days to walk, and almost 9000 people make the journey each year. Most people walk the trail between November and April, but it is possible to hike in any season.

Cradle Mountain 1545 m
Mount Emmett 1432 m
Barn Bluff 1559 m
N
0 5 10 15 20 25
KILOMETRES
the Overland Track
AUSTRALIA
Mount Pelion 1560 m
Mount Pelion East 1461 m
Mount Ossa 1617 m
TASMANIA
Mount Gould 1410 m
Mount Ida 1241 m
Mount Olympus 1449 m
Mount Hugel 1403 m
Mount Rufus 1416 m

The Overland Track is located in Tasmania, Australia.

The Overland Track is full of fascinating natural sights. It passes through an area that was once covered in ice and enormous glaciers. As the glaciers carved their way towards the sea, they left behind **craggy** rocks and rugged peaks, such as Cradle Mountain. Clear **tarns**, deep gorges and waterfalls can be found along the way. There are also wide areas of **buttongrass**, which formed after the early Indigenous people burnt forest to create hunting areas.

The Overland Track is in a region that is home to kangaroos, wombats, platypuses, echidnas and Tasmanian devils, as well as native birds, such as black cockatoos. There are also colourful wildflowers growing along the track.

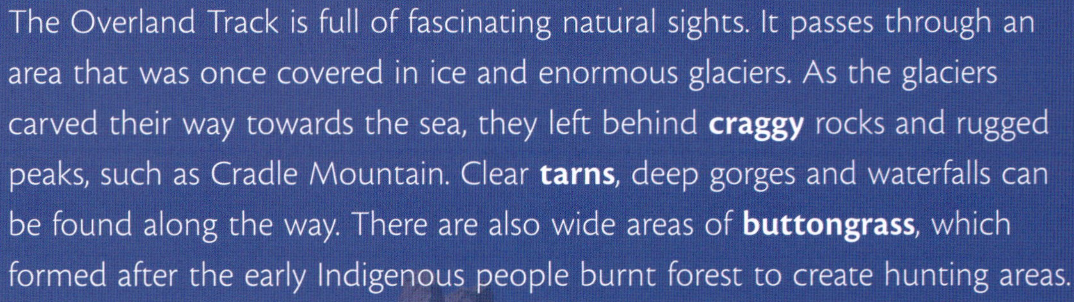

Think and Talk About ...

Indigenous Australians lived in the area of the Overland Track for more than 10 000 years.

Hikers on the Overland Track have to cross rocky areas.

Hikers have to pitch their tents on special platforms.

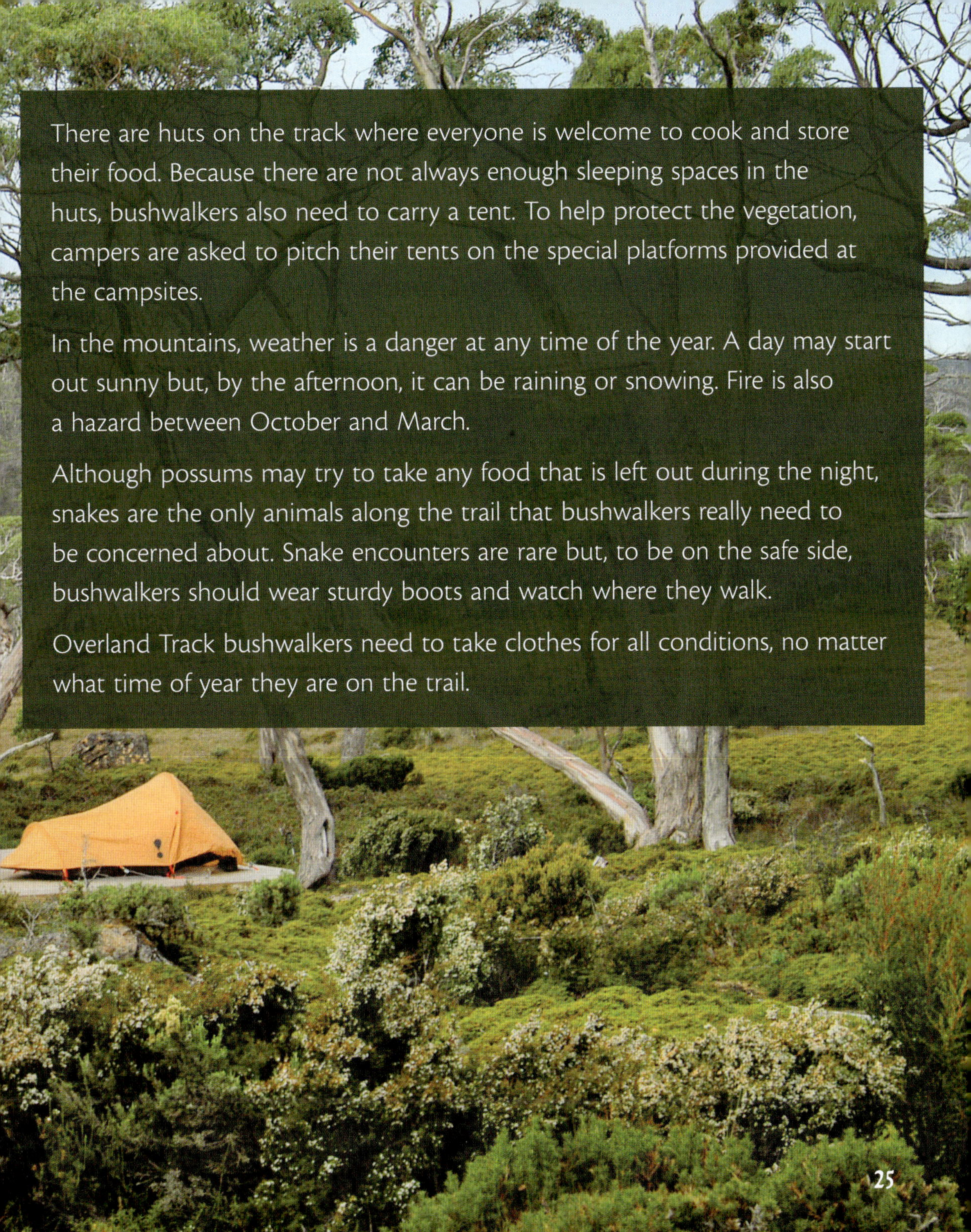

There are huts on the track where everyone is welcome to cook and store their food. Because there are not always enough sleeping spaces in the huts, bushwalkers also need to carry a tent. To help protect the vegetation, campers are asked to pitch their tents on the special platforms provided at the campsites.

In the mountains, weather is a danger at any time of the year. A day may start out sunny but, by the afternoon, it can be raining or snowing. Fire is also a hazard between October and March.

Although possums may try to take any food that is left out during the night, snakes are the only animals along the trail that bushwalkers really need to be concerned about. Snake encounters are rare but, to be on the safe side, bushwalkers should wear sturdy boots and watch where they walk.

Overland Track bushwalkers need to take clothes for all conditions, no matter what time of year they are on the trail.

It is best to walk the trail with another person but, if travelling alone, it is essential to take a **personal locator beacon (PLB)**. These beacons can be hired from the Parks and Wildlife Service. Before leaving home, bushwalkers should tell a friend where they plan to walk. They should also write their plans in a "trip intentions" logbook. These books can be found at the start of the track and in each hut along the way.

People hiking alone should take a personal locator beacon (PLB).

Think and Talk About ...

The Pacific Crest Trail, which runs from Mexico to California, in the USA, is the longest hiking trail in the world.

Be Prepared

Whether it is hiking in the USA, walking in the UK, tramping in New Zealand or bushwalking in Australia, there are many exciting trails to discover. Remember to learn as much as possible about a trail before leaving home, and be well prepared, so that the trip is safe and enjoyable.

Dove Lake Circuit

To: Clifton.Bushwalkers@tjc.com
Subject: Dove Lake Circuit

Hi Bushwalkers

If anyone in the club is interested in an enjoyable walk, I certainly recommend Dove Lake Circuit in Cradle Mountain-Lake St. Clair National Park. My family and I walked this 6-kilometre-long track in the school holidays when we were visiting Tasmania. Although it is supposed to take two hours, we were on it for three, and all of us are reasonably fit. Some parts of the circuit are steep, but there are also easier sections where there are boardwalks.

It's important to take warm clothes on the Dove Lake Circuit because it is mountainous country. Dove Lake is at an **altitude** of 934 metres. Even if the weather is fine and sunny when you start out, it can be unpredictable and change at any time. We wore runners because that's all we had with us on holiday but, if it rains, the track can get muddy and slippery. If you have boots, make sure you pack them!

Dove Lake is amazing. It was completely calm when we were there, and the mountains were reflected in the water. The lake was formed thousands of years ago when a massive glacier gouged an enormous basin out of the rock. When the glacier melted, some of the water remained in the basin and formed the lake.

The rocks around Dove Lake appear to have stripes in them. My mum is a geography teacher, and she explained that glaciers are full of rocks that grate against the walls of the valley as the glacier slowly moves downhill. The stripes are the marks left by this movement.

I am aware that some members of our bushwalking club are fascinated with animals, and that's another reason to walk the Dove Lake Circuit. On our excursion, we saw a family of wombats grazing quite close to the boardwalk and they didn't move away, even when they spotted us. We also glimpsed some wallabies bounding off into the distance. When we arrived back at the car park, some people we met said they'd seen three echidnas sitting in the grass around the edge of the lake in the sunshine. There are also supposed to be Tasmanian devils in the area. These animals are native to Tasmania, but you're not likely to see them unless you're camping overnight, because they are nocturnal.

There were some very interesting trees on the walk, many of which I didn't recognise. We photographed several and used reference books back at our accommodation to identify them. My favourite trees were the myrtle beeches in an area called the "Ballroom Forest". Some of them are so covered in moss it's almost impossible to see their bark. It's as if they're covered in a soft, green blanket. Myrtle trees can't survive in extreme forest fires, but they do grow again from seed. I guess the trees in the Ballroom Forest haven't been **ravaged** by fire for a long time, because many of them are large and well established.

We were fortunate to have had good weather for our Dove Lake bushwalk. However, I definitely recommend that you go even if it is raining because, in those conditions, you'd see waterfalls streaming down the rock walls, and water dripping off the trees.

Hopefully, I have **convinced** you that the Dove Lake Circuit is an excellent bushwalk. The Dove Lake Circuit is very popular and thousands of people walk it each year. I do hope you have an opportunity to walk the track, and if you are interested in any more information or have any questions, just email me.

Bushwalker Jac

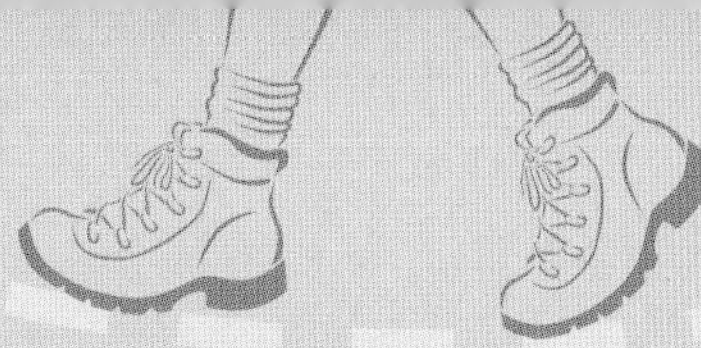

Glossary

active (*adjective*)	still working
altitude (*noun*)	the height above sea level
bothy (*noun*)	a small hut or cottage
buttongrass (*noun*)	a grass-like plant that is native to Australia
cairns (*noun*)	piles of carefully placed stones
convinced (*verb*)	persuaded people that something is true
craggy (*adjective*)	rough and uneven
gale (*noun*)	a very strong wind
gorges (*noun*)	deep, narrow valleys
hazard (*noun*)	a thing that is dangerous
moorland (*noun*)	a large area of land where there are few trees
paint blazes (*noun*)	rectangles of paint that help hikers find their way
peaks (*noun*)	the tops of mountains
personal locator beacon (PLB) (*noun*)	a device carried by hikers that helps them to be found if they become lost
ravaged (*verb*)	to be destroyed
scenic (*adjective*)	amazing to look at
tarns (*noun*)	mountain lakes
through-hike (*verb*)	to hike from one end of a trail to the other
volcanic (*adjective*)	an area of volcanoes

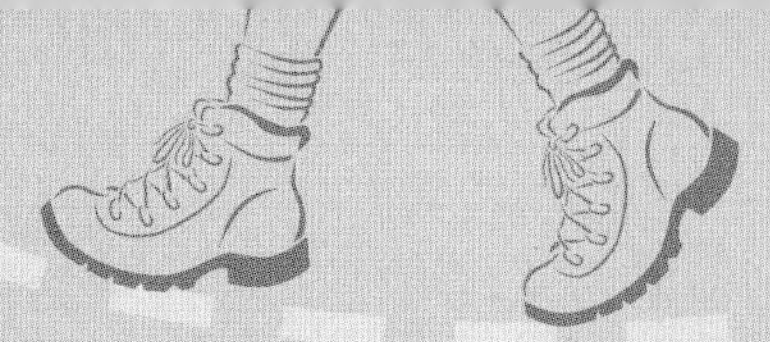

Index